Undersea Mystery Club

Trouble with Treasure

Illustrated by **Melanie Demmer**

Andrews McMeel
PUBLISHING®

Andrews McMeel Publishing
a division of Andrews McMeel Universal
1130 Walnut Street, Kansas City, Missouri 64106

www.andrewsmcmeel.com

Epic! Creations, Inc.
702 Marshall Street, Suite 280, Redwood City, California 94063

www.getepic.com

19 20 21 22 23 SDB 10 9 8 7 6 5 4 3 2 1

Paperback ISBN: 978-1-5248-5572-7
Hardback ISBN: 978-1-5248-5784-4

Library of Congress Control Number: 2019950079

Design by Wendy Gable and Dan Nordskog

Made by:
King Yip (Dongguan) Printing & Packaging Factory Ltd.
Address and location of manufacturer:
Daning Administrative District, Humen Town
Dongguan Guangdong, China 523930
1st Printing—12/23/19

For my mermaid friends,
Natalie and Caroline,
keep exploring!
—CBC

It was Spring Cleaning Day in Aquamarina, and all of the undersea city was busy dusting, sweeping, and tidying. The sun was shining and seaflowers were blooming outside of Violet's window, but she was stuck inside until her room was clean.

"If only mermaids had magical powers," she said to Dusty, the starfish that lived on her hair. "Then I could snap my fingers, and the whole place would be clean."

Lately, Violet had been spending all of her free time reading about pirates and shipwrecks. That was why her room had gotten so messy.

She sighed and picked

ATLAS

up a library book called *Atlas to Aquamarina.* It was filled with maps, including one of Pinnacle Point, which was the oldest part of the city.

Tap tap tap!

Someone was knocking at her bedroom door.

"Come in," Violet yelled.

A young narwhal with a long ivory tusk appeared in her doorway.

"Wally!" Violet was thrilled

to have a surprise visit from her best friend.

"Hey, Violet," Wally replied. "Whatcha doing?" He swam into the room carefully, trying to avoid a giant pile of clothes. "Want to play tide-and-seek?"

"Yeah!" Violet exclaimed. It was one of her favorite games. One creature would hide, and then the other would look for them. "But I have to clean my room first."

"Okay," Wally said. He took a bag of seagrass cookies out of his backpack.

"Want one?" he asked.

"Sure!" Violet replied, catching the cookie he tossed her way.

Violet's mom, the mayor of Aquamarina, peeked into the room.

"Hi, you two," she said with

a smile. “How’s the tidying up going?”

Violet looked at the papers overflowing her desk, toys scattered all across her floor, and laundry pile that had been there so long that it might be home to new life-forms.

“I think I like summer, fall, and winter dirtying more than I like spring cleaning," she said.

"I can help!" Wally offered. "The two of us together can get it done twice as fast." He used his tusk to swipe a bunch of puzzle pieces off of a table and back into their box.

Violet smiled. Any friend could help make a mess, but only the best kind of friend would help clean one up.

"Looks like you're off to a good start," her mom said. "I'll be back in a bit to collect anything you want to donate."

"Okay, let's do this!" Violet said, getting a second wind. She tossed a bunch of drawings, sports medals, and baby pictures into a bin. Together, she and Wally worked to get the room back in order.

Within an hour, the room was spotless. (Well, almost spotless. Violet's comforter was covered in polka dots.)

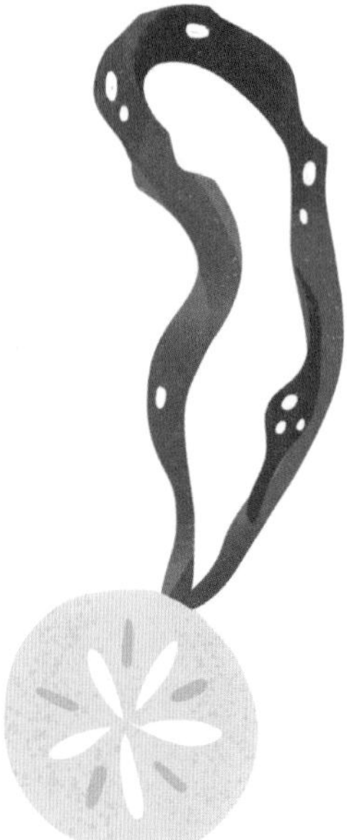

Violet's mom came back into the room with a box labeled Donations.

"Looks great!" she said. "Before you go outside,

You're fin-tastic

do you have anything you want to give away?"

"Yes!" Violet replied. She pointed to the bin of photos, medals, and drawings.

Her mom frowned.

"Why are you getting rid of these things?" she asked, sorting through the pile. "They bring back lots of great memories."

"Ugh," Violet groaned. "I'm too old for this stuff, Mom."

“But you might want it someday,” her mother replied. “History is important, and our past helps us better understand who we are.”

She smiled as she held up a baby picture of Violet and Wally.

"Well, I won't tell you what is or isn't important to you," she said. "But just think about it some more before you get rid of this stuff for good."

"I will," Violet said. But as soon as her mom left, she stuffed the *Atlas to Aquamarina* book into her backpack and motioned for Wally to follow her out the door.

It was time to explore!

Violet and Wally swam out into the cool, crisp water. All over town, ocean creatures were cleaning out their shops and homes. All of the stores, except the restaurants, were cleaning out the buildings where they lived and worked.

"I want to show you something," Violet said. She swerved to avoid a pile of recycling near the curb.

"What?" Wally asked.

"Follow me! I want it to be a surprise."

They swam through town. Along the way, they passed the school, the village hall, the library, and the new playground that they had helped build a couple of weeks before. Fish of all sizes squealed as they played on the shiny new equipment.

They swam and swam and swam some more.

"Are we almost there?" Wally asked.

"Almost!" Violet replied.

They kept swimming. The water got colder and the shadows grew longer until they were on the outskirts of the city.

Finally, when Wally thought he couldn't swim any farther,

Violet shouted, “We’re here!”

“Where is ‘here,’ exactly?” he asked. It looked to him like the spot they’d come to was totally abandoned.

“Pinnacle Point,” Violet replied. “The earliest-known part of Aquamarina. Not to mention

the perfect place for tide-and-seek! Isn't it cool?"

Wally shivered.

"Literally," he said.

Violet laughed.

"I'll hide and you seek!" she said. "This will be home base." She pointed to a large rock near

a clearing.

Wally covered his eyes with his flippers and began to count to thirty.

"One, two, three, four, five, six, seven, eight, nine—"

"You're counting too fast!" Violet interrupted.

"Oops!" he said. "I'll start over."

"One...two...three...four..."

"Now you're counting too slow!"

"Okay," Wally replied. "I'll count more medium."

Wally began to count more medium, and Violet swam off as quickly as she could. She kept count along with Wally until she could no longer hear him. Then she started counting along in her head.

Violet passed by several good hiding spots, hoping to find the very *best* one. She soon found herself deep in the underwater

trenches. She passed a big, dark cave. It was the ideal hiding spot!

Violet crouched down just inside the mouth of the cave and waited.

"This is perfect!" she whispered.

"Perfect!" repeated Dusty.

"Shhh!" she reminded him.

"Shhh!" he repeated loudly.

Violet had to cover her mouth to stop giggling.

Several minutes passed with no sign of Wally. Violet was so

well hidden that she started to get impatient.

"Maybe I can do a little exploring while I wait," she said to herself.

Violet looked around. Only a small sliver of sunlight shone into the cave, so it was very hard to see how far back it went. She reached into her backpack and pulled out a flashlight.

Violet wondered how long it

had been since anyone had been inside this cave. The walls were shiny and smooth from the ocean water. There were rock formations hanging from the ceiling and reaching up from the ground. Violet started swimming toward the back of the cave when she stubbed her fin on something.

"Ouch!" she grumbled, looking down. Something was lodged in the sand. With her flashlight shining on the object, she could

make out a hard wooden corner.

"Maybe it's a treasure chest!" she exclaimed.

"Maybe!" Dusty agreed.

Violet grabbed a flat shell and began to dig as quickly as she could. Once more of the object was revealed, she realized that it was a box with shiny metal hinges and a large lock on the front. She had definitely found something special.

Wally had been looking in the same spots over and over, trying to find Violet. By now, he knew she wasn't hiding in any of them, but he didn't want to stray too far from home base and risk getting lost—or worse!

CLUNK!

A loud noise in the distance caught Wally's attention. He pictured a giant sea monster stomping toward him, ready to attack. He squeezed his eyes shut. But after a minute passed and he didn't get gobbled up, he realized that it must be something else.

CLUNK!

Hmm, he thought.

CLUNK!

What could that noise possibly be? (Wally didn't have to think out loud because he didn't have a starfish living on his head.)

Wally didn't really want

to investigate, but he knew that if he'd heard a loud, weird sound, Violet had probably heard it, too. She would *definitely* want to investigate, so finding that noise was his best chance of finding her.

He gathered up his courage and swam toward the clunking sound.

Wally followed the noise to a big, dark cave deep in the ocean.

Maybe it's coming from a sea monster after all, Wally worried.

"Violet?" he whispered.

No response.

"Violet?" he called a little louder.

Still no response.

"Violet?" he yelled at the top of his lungs.

"Wally!" Violet shouted. "I'm here! Help me!"

"I'm coming!" Wally called back. He was very scared, but if his best friend was in trouble, he had no time to hesitate.

Wally rushed into the cave. He found Violet in a deep hole, next to an unusual object.

"Are you okay?" Wally asked.

"Are you trapped in that hole?"

"I'm okay, and I'm not trapped," Violet replied. "But I found something!"

She shined her flashlight on the object.

Wally saw a mysterious wooden box with a giant metal lock on the front.

"What is *that*?" he asked. He was confused, but also relieved that Violet wasn't in trouble.

"I think it's a treasure chest!

But I can't be sure without opening it. I tried knocking the lock off with a shell, but it wouldn't budge."

Wally's eyes widened.

"A treasure chest in Aquamarina? How exciting!"

"Yeah!" Violet agreed. "And I need your help getting it out of here. It's wedged in."

"Okay," Wally said. He used his tusk to help dig out the box.

With one big tug, they pulled it free from the sand.

The chest's wood was splintered and gray. Shiny metal hardware held it together tightly.

"Hmm," Violet said, checking

the lock. “It’s locked.”

Violet tugged on the lock, but it held fast.

“Let me try,” Wally said. “I can use my tusk like a key.”

Wally put his tusk into the keyhole, but the lock

still wouldn't budge.

"We'll have to try something else," Violet said.

Wally shivered.

"This place gives me the creeps," he said. "We should take the box somewhere else and try to open it there."

Violet nodded, smiling. "Do you know where?"

"To the clubhouse!" they yelled together.

Violet and Wally's secret clubhouse was hidden in a small alcove in the middle of a coral reef outside of town. It was where they always did their very best mystery-solving.

Bringing the chest to the

clubhouse wasn't easy, but they caught an ocean current on the way back to Aquamarina, which made the box a lot easier to carry. Soon they were comfortably lounging in their clubhouse sand chairs.

"Ready for a brainstorm?" Violet asked, taking out her trusty hourglass and notepad.

A brainstorm was when the best friends came up with a bunch of ideas or possible solutions to whatever problem they were facing.

"Yep!" Wally said. He flipped her a pencil with his tusk. "I have so many questions! How can we open the box? Who put this box together? What could be in it?"

What could be in the box? Violet wrote at the top of her notebook page. She turned over the hourglass.

"I'll go first," Violet said. With a grunt, she tried to lift the box.

“Treasure, jewels, gold coins, a million seagrass cookies...” The ideas were coming to her so quickly that it was hard to write them all down. Finally, she put down her pencil and stopped to breathe.

“What do *you* think is in the box?” she asked Wally.

Wally had some ideas, too. Violet picked up the pencil again.

“Tons of homework, vegetables, narwhal-eating monsters…”

“I hope it’s one of my ideas and

not one of yours," Violet interrupted. "And there's only one way to find out: Open the chest and see if we are right. But to do that, we need to think outside the box."

"We're already outside the box!" Wally said.

Violet laughed. "No, thinking 'outside the box' means thinking creatively."

"Oh!" Wally said. "Like, go back in time to ask the person who put it there if we can borrow the key?"

Violet smiled. "Maybe that's a little *too far* outside the box."

"Or invent X-ray glasses to see inside?" he asked.

Violet laughed and waved her hands.

"Or drop a huge boulder on top so that the box breaks into a million pieces?"

Violet clutched her sides, laughing.

"Not quite. I think we should find someone who can pick a lock," she replied.

"Good idea," Wally said. "How about Mr. Finn, the town locksmith?"

"His shop is closed for Spring Cleaning Day," Violet reminded him.

"Right. How about Ms. Pearl, the hardware store owner?"

Violet shook her head. "Her place is closed, too."

The last grain of sand slipped through the hourglass, but Violet wasn't going to stop thinking until they had a plan.

"We'll have to find someone else to pick the lock," Wally said.

“Gill can do it!” Violet shouted, clapping her hands together.

As always, their brainstorm had helped them come up with a plan.

Gill Sharkfin was the biggest troublemaker in town. If anyone could pick a lock, it was him. In fact, for the last Aquamarina Town Prank Day (a holiday Gill had made up, of course), he had switched all of the locks to the stores on Main Street. All of the shop owners were locked out of their businesses, and everyone was furious. (Well, everyone except Mr. Finn, who ended up with a whole lot of unexpected business that day.)

Violet and Wally lugged the chest all the way to the Shark Fin Diner, the restaurant Gill's parents owned. Gill sometimes worked there on weekends. "Sometimes" meant that he had been hired and fired—and rehired and refired—more times than anyone could keep track of, including Gill and his parents. As a result, no one ever really knew whether he was supposed to show up for work or not, which was exactly the way Gill liked it.

Violet and Wally found Gill behind the counter, switching the contents of the ketchup and mustard bottles.

"What's up?" he asked. "And what's *that*?"

The large wooden box had immediately caught his attention.

"Hey, Gill," Violet said as she plunked the box down on the counter with a thud. "We have a lock we want you to pick for us."

She pointed to the large lock. Gill took a look and then shrugged.

"You know," he said, "it's a lot less fun when you actually *want* me to do it. Plus, as you can see, I'm pretty busy over here." He screwed the top back onto a ketchup bottle that he'd just filled with mustard.

"No problem," Violet replied, winking at Wally. "If you think you can't do it, it's no big—"

"Wait!" Gill interrupted, spilling mustard on the counter. "Of course I *could* do it, if I wanted to."

"I don't know," Violet said with a smirk. "It looks like a pretty hard one."

"No way!" Gill replied. "I could do it, easy peasy. Let me get my

lock-picking set."

Violet smiled at Wally as Gill reached into his backpack.

"You mean you have it with you right now?" Wally asked, surprised.

"Of course," Gill replied. He pulled out two small metal tools and immediately started working on the lock.

Violet and Wally waited as Gill tried to open the lock. As the minutes ticked by, he grew more and more frustrated. For some

reason, it just wouldn't open. After a while, he stopped and wiped his brow.

"I hate to tell you this," Gill said, "but this lock is too old for me to pick. You're not going to be able to open it without the original key."

Violet sighed. It wasn't what she wanted to hear, but that was okay. She definitely wasn't giving up. If there was one thing she had learned, it was that you always have to keep trying if you want to be a really good problem-solver.

Suddenly, the bell on the front door rang. Violet, Wally, and Gill saw a customer walk into the restaurant.

"Gotta go," Gill said, grabbing the condiment bottles. "*Ketchup* with you two later."

The customer, a green sea turtle, came in and took a seat at the counter right next to Violet and Wally.

Violet recognized her as Clara Reed, the town historian. Clara ran the local museum and sometimes worked with Violet's mom to plan town events.

"Hi, Clara," Violet said.

"Hi, Violet. Hi, Wally," she said with a smile. She looked over at Gill and narrowed her eyes. "Hello, Gilliam."

(The museum's lock had also been switched the year before, and Clara had definitely *not* forgotten who was to blame.)

"What are you all *up to*?" she asked, looking pointedly at Gill.

Gill smiled widely and handed

her a menu. “May I suggest an order of fries?” he asked, placing the mustard and ketchup bottles in front of her.

Clara looked at the bottles suspiciously.

“I’ll have a seaweed salad,” she said. “What are you two having?”

“We’re actually here on a mission,” Violet replied. She patted the wooden box on the counter. “We found this treasure chest in the trenches outside

Aquamarina, and we're trying to get it open."

Clara put on the glasses that were hanging around her neck and looked at the box more closely.

"Why, I can't believe it!" she exclaimed.

"It wasn't me!" Gill yelled from the other side of the restaurant.

"Not you," Clara said, waving him off. "This box! You found the lost time capsule of Aquamarina!"

"The what?" Wally asked.

"A time capsule is a container full of important items from a very long time ago," she explained. "This one is more than 100 years old! Most of our early town records and artifacts, including the map showing the location of this time capsule, were lost years ago when an earthquake destroyed the original town hall. No one has been able to locate it since—until today!"

Violet and Wally exchanged glances.

"We thought it was full of buried treasure," Violet said, trying to hide her disappointment.

"This is even more precious than buried treasure, Violet," Clara said. "It contains a rare look into the past, and our town's history. For so long, much of our history was a big question mark, but you just discovered a box full of answers!"

Violet smiled. That actually sounded pretty neat.

"But we can't get it open," Wally reminded them. "We need the original key."

"Leave that to me," Clara said, clapping her hands.

The next day, Mayor Vespera and Clara hosted a History Day event at the local museum. Everyone in town gathered in the main hall to watch the opening of the time capsule.

As it turned out, the key to the chest had been on display in the museum for many years, right alongside a plaque reading, "Key to the Lost Time Capsule of Aquamarina." The key was one of the few items that had been salvaged after the earthquake.

"More than 100 years ago," Clara began, "the founders of our beloved Aquamarina came together to create this time capsule on the day they named the town. Today, we honor our past, celebrate our present, and look with hope to our future."

When she said, "our future," she handed Violet and Wally a heavy gold key.

"Go ahead and open it," she said. "You were the explorers who made this great discovery possible."

Violet and Wally beamed and inserted the key into the lock together.

“On three,” Wally said, adding, “and make sure you count medium!”

Violet laughed.

“One...two...three!”

Click!

The lock popped open.

The hinges on the wooden box creaked. Violet felt her heart pounding. She had promised herself that she would find a way to open the chest, and she had finally done it.

Inside the time capsule were lots of loose papers and photographs. Violet looked more closely. There were letters from family members to their loved ones, marriage and birth certificates, and a book called a register that listed every person who lived in town on the day the capsule was sealed. Each item contained valuable information about the founding of

the town.

Wally noticed some shiny coins scattered among the papers. “Looks like we found some gold after all!” Wally said, nudging Violet.

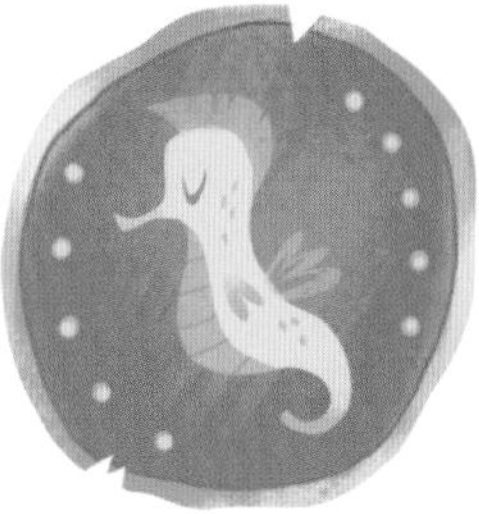

The coins were exciting, but it was a photograph near the top of the chest that caught Violet’s eye. Two sea creatures were smiling and holding hands. One of them held the register that was in the time capsule now. It reminded Violet of her brainstorming notebook.

"Looks like the founders of our town were good friends, too,"

Mayor Vespera said, putting her arms around Violet and Wally. “I’m so proud of your hard work, and I’m so happy that you’re both starting to understand the importance of history.”

“You’re right,” Violet replied. “And that gives me an idea!”

The Found Time Capsule of Aquamarina

Aquamarina

After the ceremony ended, Clara and her team put the contents of the time capsule on display in the museum for everyone in town to see. They even updated the plaque to read, "The *Found* Time Capsule of Aquamarina."

Violet invited Wally back to hang out in her newly clean bedroom and hear her idea.

"Let's create our own time capsule!" Violet said.

"That's a great idea!" Wally replied.

Violet fished an old box out of her closet and stenciled **Best Friends Time Capsule** in big, dark letters on top.

"Now what should we include?"

she asked, pulling off the lid.

“Do you have any more seagrass cookies?” Wally asked.

“Seagrass cookies?” Violet responded. “Those won’t last long enough!”

“Oh, they’re not for the time

capsule," Wally replied, rubbing his tummy with his flippers.

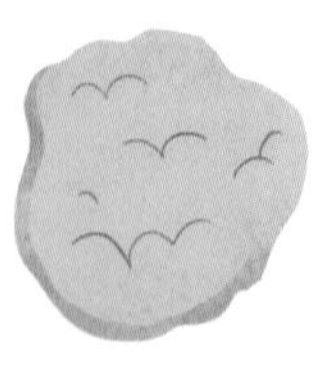

Violet chuckled and tossed him a couple of cookies from a nearby tray. Then she was off, rummaging through all of the things she

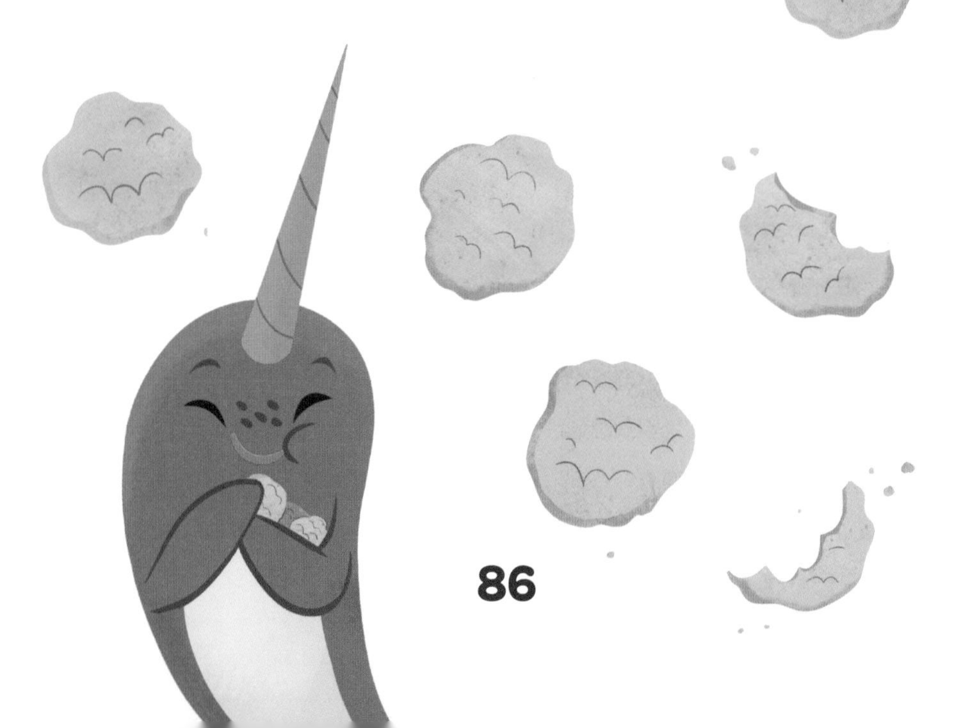

had been ready to give away the day before.

"I know exactly what I want to include," Violet said. She gathered up her favorite items from their past and placed them in the box. She included some old report cards, a second-place medal from the town spelling bee, and friendship bracelets that she and Wally had made long ago. On top, she put the photograph of her and Wally when they were babies.

“To honor our past,” she said. “And to celebrate our present.”

Violet and Wally posed to take a picture together and then added the photo to the box.

“That should do it,” Wally said. “Anything else?”

"Yes!" Violet told him. She picked up the front page of the local newspaper, the *Aquamarina Times,* and placed it on top of the pile.

"I love it!" Wally said.

"Me too," Violet said. She put the lid back on the box.

Violet and Wally carried their time capsule outside. They dug a big hole in the sand in Violet's backyard. They placed the box in the hole and covered it with sand. When they were done, Violet put a big rock on top so they'd remember where it was buried.

"When do we open it?" Wally asked.

“Let’s do it in ten years,” Violet replied.

“Deal!”

It felt good to know that their memories, like their friendship, would be around for a long, long time.

Undersea Mystery Club

More to Explore

True Undersea Mysteries

Real Sunken Treasure

Sunken treasure really does exist! When ships sink, the items onboard may fall to the bottom of the ocean, where they stay until they are recovered by historians, archaeologists, or explorers.

One example of this is the

wreck of the *San José*. In 1708, the Spanish galleon sank off the coast of Colombia. The ship, which was loaded with gold, silver, and emeralds, was discovered not long ago by a robotic submarine.

Our vast oceans haven't been explored completely, so there could still be sunken treasure waiting to be found!

Preserving the Past

Who Are Historians?

Historians are experts who learn about the past. They study all kinds of material, including artifacts, photographs, and documents from a specific time period.

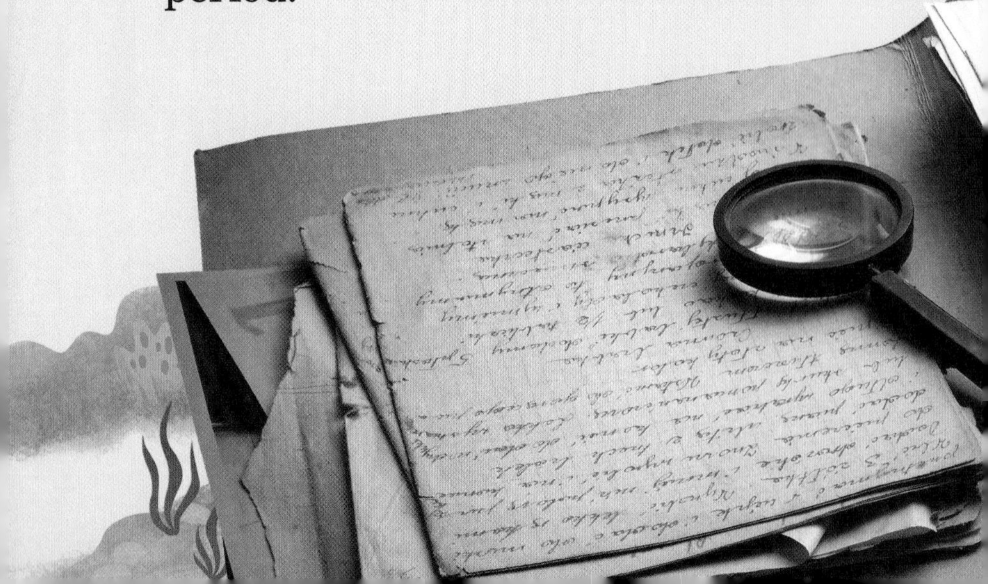

Historians help people know more about their towns by giving presentations and creating interesting and informative museum displays.

Maybe someday you can be a historian and share your knowledge of the past!

Build Your Own Time Capsule

Create your own time capsule, just like Violet and Wally!

1. Pick your treasure, such as journals, toys, pictures, clothes, and newspaper clippings.
2. Choose a container that's large enough to hold everything.

3. Add your items to the container, and include a letter explaining your time capsule.
4. Seal your time capsule with tape or glue and put it in a place where it won't be disturbed.
5. Plan a time to open it, whether in a year or fifty. It will be fun to rediscover your treasure!

About the Author

Courtney Carbone studied English and creative writing in the United States and Australia before becoming a children's book writer and editor in New York City. Her favorite things include trivia nights, board games, stand-up comedy, bookstores, brick-oven pizza, and sharks.

About the Illustrator

Melanie Demmer attended the College for Creative Studies in Detroit, where she earned a BFA in illustration. Currently based in Los Angeles, she creates artwork digitally but also enjoys using watercolors, markers, colored pencils, and acrylic paints. Melanie loves to create bright, colorful illustrations with a variety of textures.

Look for more adventures with the

Undersea Mystery Club

COMING SOON!